# Twilight

## ...the in-between

## Linda L. Flynn
*jouneytotheheights.com*

ISBN: 978-1-7321864-5-3

## DEDICATION

**Twilight …the in-between** is dedicated to all who recognize the reality of "in-between" spaces and are ready to embrace the "twilight" within their lives.

If you don't think you are there yet,
…you may be surprised to find yourself there
after reading this book.

.

# CONTENTS

# ACKNOWLEDGMENTS

There are so many who have influenced and encouraged me in this work. Many thanks go to the Irish writers I first met in 2019, and those who I continue to meet with weekly. This group of writers encouraged me to release the muse of poetry I had locked away so many years ago. The larger group was "the Leslie Collins Writing Group of Tralee." Within that group, I had the opportunity to work with Maire Holmes, who told me my work was poetry long before I could recognize it as such. Leslie, Judy, Mary and Joan remain committed to meeting regularly via technology. Barbara helped with my punctuation editing and layout formatting. More locally, my friend Jane tells me my poetry has opened her eyes to the relevance of poetry. Danielle, Beth, Christa and Francesca all touch base with me regularly to ensure I'm still writing. My husband is steadfast in his support of the time I steal away to write, edit or listen to some training session.

I fear I forgot to mention some, but please know that I appreciate the encouragement and accountability you have offered.

A special thanks to all who share my work with their friends.

# Definition

## Twilight as a noun

A soft, diffused light from the sky when the sun is below the horizon, either from daybreak to sunrise, or more commonly, from sunset to nightfall

The period in the morning or in the evening during which this light prevails

An intermediate state that is not clearly defined

e.g., lived in the twilight of neutrality.

A state of uncertainty, vagueness, or gloom

A period of decline

A terminal period, especially after full development, success, etc.

e.g., in the twilight of his life.

## Twilight as an adjective

Of, relating to, or resembling twilight; dim; obscure

e.g., In the twilight hours.

Appearing or flying at twilight; crepuscular

Linda L. Flynn

# Introducing Twilight

...the in-between

Life is a series of twilight experiences.
One may recognize this state when expecting something forthcoming
Or dreading the onset of an event or marker in time.

What we often cannot recognize
Is that life happens in the twilight zone.
One is constantly moving toward something,
At the same time, leaving something else.

Throughout life, we move from one stage to another
Sometimes eagerly, other times begrudgingly

Business moves from creation to success or failure
Relationships shift from introduction to something meaningful or
Something to run from

Cultures too.

Though many cannot accept this condition.
They cling desperately to distorted memories of the past,
Despising where they currently find themselves.

The tug-of-war begins—
Those trying to go back in time
Against those trying to rush forward,
With few, content to live in the now.

And so,
We live in the tension of these days.
All the emotions stirred by twilight
Exist in some form or another.
All being acted out
Some in the public square, some privately.

Some might construe our current events as farcical,
if they weren't so dark and oppressive.
Yet times will change, as they do
Something new will arise
Schedule,
Unknown to all.

I believe a phoenix will rise from the ashes
One always does,
Though rarely meeting our timetable,
Or even the way we expected it to.

This book, is a collection of writings
Relating to various twilight times in life.
Some bleak, others hopeful.
You may relate to some of these in-between times,
Or not.
Either way,
I hope you'll enjoy my musings.

# RELATIONAL

# Spiraling

*(Published on The Galway Review site on 9/20/2023)*

Laying in the shade
Recalling the previous weeks
Life was spinning!
Spinning!
Faster!
And faster!
Like a carnival ride
Taking me into oblivion.

With each added weight
Speed accelerates.
Focus gone.
Head heavy.
Breathing labored.

Flung from the ride and thrust into the sea
The weight of what life has
Thrown at me, carries me
Deeper and deeper.

Shaking free,
The ascent begins.
Then, breaking the surface
Gasping for air—
No focus.

Waves are pushing,
Gently guiding towards shore.

Treading water,
Feeling weightless,
Rolling towards the shore.

You threw out a lifeline,
And then another.
Friends stood on the beach
Cheering me back to solid ground.

Exhausted I was,
Yet there we were found, dancing with joy.
Life without friends is barely life at all.

My heart no longer pounding.

# Tension

*(Published on The Galway Review site on 9/20/2023)*

Unaware
yet always there,
the tension between life and death.

Oblivious
we go about our days.

Age
Fragility
Illness
remind us otherwise,
or in an instant someone is snatched away.

Survivors
or those left behind
have various ways of dealing with this loss.

Excuses or justification,
saying words which help no one.
Or,
refusing to speak of the departed anymore.

Some are stuck in the pit of emptiness
left by their passing.

These mortal bodies are home for only a season,
yet we become so attached to them.
They provide the comfort of all we've known
and the essence by which we are known to others.

Despite knowing the body is temporary
we fail to learn the language for gracefully saying goodbye,
to both our own and those of others.

Immortal we think.
Knowing only life
as we wander this earth.

# Friends

Like a breeze, blowing through a room
the cobwebs blew out of my mind.

Being awakened from a dream
thoughts regained form and color,

nothing changed,
life and death hang in the balance.

We seldom acknowledge
how intertwined they are.

Awakening after a long hibernation,
inhaling and feeling the force of life

now flowing through my lungs and
coursing through my body,

I've returned to life.

With a recognition of those who held me
while feeling heavy and dark,

comes the knowledge of power we carry
when we share life and friendship.

# Where I'm From

I am from the womb of my mother
carefully knit together by the loving hands of the heavenly Father.
Deposited into my parents' arms that early morning on January seventh.

My mother is relieved I am here
My father, disappointed I am not his coveted son
And so, life begins with a close extended maternal family and very distant
paternal one.

Seeds of creativity dropped on me early
swirling through the atmosphere, watered by
family, close friends, and neighbors.

Words crafted, create images in my mind
carrying me to unknown places.
Planting yet other seeds which grow
into the desire to travel and explore different cultures.

Always in the background is the nagging sensation,
I am not enough
not perfect
not the desired one.

Those bulbs, if allowed to grow, can almost choke out anything
worthwhile.

Kind teachers, grandparents, and a neighbor who becomes like a mentor
keep tossing in seeds, encouraging creativity, life, and exploration.
Books keep taking me away
and away
and away.

And away I go.

Eventually I learn to tend my own garden
and find the skills to remove those weeds
which have flourished for so long.
In pulling weeds,
I also toss some folks from my life.

Scary stuff and much hard work.

Now those images are so far back in the past
They are barely visible anymore.

The scars they leave on my heart allow me
to be sensitive to the suffering of others.

After the hard work of the night,
there is life and light.

This is what I reflect.

It is who I am.

# Helpless

Restaurant patrons froze.
He became louder and more agitated
Threatening to burn the establishment
And all inside.
Others seated with him
Scurried to usher him out.

Grandchildren share stories of concern.
Tales of what they have witnessed
His uncontrollable anger and desire to punish others
His wife rues the situation yet knows not how to flee.

Family speaks of the need for him to be controlled.
Where can they go for help?

In truth,
There is nowhere,
Unless he commits himself —
Few law enforcement personnel will take action
Until he has caused some catastrophic event.
Who will be the victim before the family speaks out,
Or the authorities haul him away?

Will anyone bear the guilt of inaction?

# Memories

*Clouds, Dreams & Fantasy Copyright 2023 by AppleWood Press*

Memories are sneaky
Minding my own business
Tall and lanky slid into the seat next to me
Me, tired and eager to get home
Him, jerking and twisting
Scanning the passengers
Jiggling his legs incessantly
Close quarters in the cabin
His actions put my senses on alert
Who was he and what was he up to
Push those thoughts away
Go back to reading
Meals served
Masks off
Conversation ensued
Eyes danced and sparkled
First trip to dream location
America
Excitement was contagious
Slumbering thoughts awakened
Forgotten emotions resurfaced
Transatlantic excitement from my twenties

# One Hot Mess

Full schedule
Sweltering heat
Tasks piling up
Little time for contemplation or writing
Deadline loomed
Words dashed onto paper
No time to review.

The group met
Apologies presented before I began.
I read my haphazard words.
Yikes!
Time distorted
Character names misused
Dialog plausible
Tension set the scene

Grace abounded.
They followed the direction for this chapter
The presented situation was conceivable

Creative friends are a gift!
They see us at our best
And our worst
Yet offer encouragement, suggestions, and friendship
I recorded their notes
And added my own stating,
One Hot Mess

I departed this meeting—
Humbled
Grateful
Confident of the friendship with these writers
And my place in this group.

# The Ticking Clock

I'm grateful my thoughts rarely migrate in this direction.
However, when youthful, arrogance raises its ugly head and strikes,
The impact leaves an indelible mark, which itself requires voice.
The clock ticks on, providing either opportunity or loss.
Sometimes, both.

A little knowledge puffs up the bravado of youth
Unchecked, the ego grows
Brazen acts often follow.

Efforts to temper or correct such behaviors are rebuffed
Self-importance inflates further until the youth believes they are
invincible.
Nothing can stop or temper one in this state.

They pick up their bow and load up their fiery darts.
Look out world—
There is an out-of-control juvenile on the prowl.

They raise their bow
Then load their darts
And randomly attack any within range.

Unsuspecting and unprepared
The injured struggle to understand what happened.

The youth
In glee
Walks away confident they just proved their point.

Their words
Like daggers
Cut quick to the bone
Gushing forth pain and disbelief at youth's indifference.

As the youth struts away
They turn with a smirk and say,
"YOU have to earn respect."

Ahhh, respect.
A word the injured knows well.
At this
The injured smiles and thinks to themself,
"Yes, respect must be earned.
You
My youthful individual
Have a long way to go before you earn my respect."

And so, as in this case, sometimes the generational gap widens.
The clock ticks on. Another day, another opportunity.

I treasure many relationships with youthful individuals.
The ones who want to explore life
Want to build
Not destroy.
With them
There is a camaraderie
A feeling we are working toward something.
There is pleasure found in time spent together.
The clock ticks on.
Opportunity or loss.
Your choice.

# Confusion

Fusion.
Confusion.
Explosion!

All retreated
Each to nurse their wounds.
Time moved on,
Relationships developed and grew.

Life continued.
The passage of time appeared to heal the wounds.

Except not,
At least for one
I learned.

For her
Pain gnawed and grew.
Maturity allowed articulate speech.
Stuck in the past
Her wounds have festered and flourished.

Confusion returned to me.

What I interpret her wanting
I cannot give—
It requires a lie.

Unable to change the past.
Unwilling to deny my happiness.

I can offer forgiveness.
I can give love.
I can overlook the offenses.

My conscience is clear.
I can move forward,
Can she?

# Love

*(Published on The Galway Review site on 9/20/2023)*

Across the table I sit,
Patio lights twinkle
Bringing light to the night
Where you gaze at me.
Your look returns me to when our love was young.
My heart melts
No words are spoken.

We sit
Soaking the comfort of the night air
And each other's company.
Where have all the days gone?
Days roll into weeks
Weeks into months
Months into years
Those years have flown by like feathers swirling in the breeze;
My heart holds them all.

Will others know of this great love,
Of the happiness we bring to one another?
If they do
Will they find it be an inspiration?
What others think matters not
It is enough that we know.

For as long as we both live,
my heart, my love,
and...
All my tomorrows are yours.

Love and time continue
Until there are no tomorrows.

I love you!

## Sorrow

Pain. I hurt.
Like sharp darts you throw words,
your anger pierces my heart.

Words, I have none,
they only fuel the flame
to restock your quiver.

Your children now grown.
for years have heard the disrespect and contempt
so frequently bestowed upon me.

My sorrow is double
First, the pain of my own heart
then for yours,
when you reap what you've sown.

Hope stirs awake the reminder.
Change is always possible.
Together, we may forge a different path for our future.

# Bittersweet

I remember the first time you brought me here.
We were visiting your California winter home.
After driving the countryside and viewing
vineyards and olive groves from twisty country roads
your hubby pulled into a parking lot.
The sun already gone for the day
left us in the dark looking at the structure.
This Spanish style building, dark,
save for the entrance lights
and those lighting the bridge to this entrance
stood stately against the night sky.
In this light, it appeared enchanting.
We entered and were seated
The environment was lively and robust
The evening consisted of great food
much conversation and laughter.
Lots of laughter.

I left with memories indelibly planted,
with no recollection of the name of the establishment
nor of the town.
Only of the fun evening shared with friends.
We returned to your home and spent another day together.

Activities created fresh memories through the years of our friendship.

Who could have predicted that several years later we would relocate?
After settling and getting accustomed to the area,
We were checking out local eateries.
Imagine my surprise when discovering this cafe is now local for me!
I go there and the memories of my first visit come flooding back.
How I would like us to retell them together.
You, now departed from this earth leave me no choice but
to savor these thoughts alone.

Thanks for the memories!

# Pearls

The original gift from the sea
Uniquely come in different sizes and colors
Once harvested, become beautiful pieces of jewelry art
Generate many emotions and memories
A single strand is elegant and simplistic
As it glides against the skin of the wearer

Pearls
Adorned my grandmother's neck.
They were her favored jewelry.
I see a strand of pearls and think of her.

In my youth, single pearls were only jewelry to me.

My first strand of pearls was gifted to me
by an employer for a work anniversary.
That's when I learned the joy of wearing pearls.

These same pearls, I lent to you
As something borrowed for your wedding day.

This first strand broke, and like any small round item,
They scattered.
I scampered to retrieve the little white globes,
Yet failed to find them all
And thought the loss of the strand was important.

But from you, I learned a different story.
To you, they were mine.
You wore them on your wedding day.
They can be worked into something uniquely different.
Keeping the pearls is more important to you than the strand.

Pearls
And so, the gift from the sea
to you is given
from me.

## Grace Personified

*(For Cindy)*

You,
Arms overflowing with gifts of the Father
Some days
Flowers,
Others love

He lifts you up
Strengthens you
Empowers you to carry the burdens of others

# EMOTIONAL

## The Big Easy

Finally,
Sitting in a quiet space
My senses are settling down.
Sifting through the exposure of this trip.

After landing in the historic, multi-cultural, metropolitan area
Sights, sounds, smells, and flavors all came together at one time.
In one place...
Constantly
Traffic never stops
Sirens punctuate the air
Music blares, escaping various doorways
Colliding with the sound of those performing in the street.
People walk these streets
Holding hands
Carrying drinks
Smoking
The smell of marijuana hangs heavy in the outside air.
Honing my senses to look beyond the surface
I find buildings designed in days gone by.
Some proudly display hanging baskets and planters overflowing with
flowers
Set against decorative metalwork balconies and entrance ways.
Others, covered with graffiti often host for-sale signs
Hoping to lure someone into the neighborhood.
Many small shops emit strong fragrances from within.
Tobacco from the cigar shop
Conflicted florals from candle shops or bodywork shops
Rivaling savory or smoky fragrances from the plethora of eateries.
All compete against the backdrop scent of overflowing garbage bins and
pot wafting through the air.
Cuisine is as varied as everything else in this city,
Showcasing the multiple cultures that settled and blended here.
Surprising
Delightful
And, so enjoyable!

I ate my way through the city, with each meal awakening different taste buds.
The people who lived or worked within the city were friendly
They genuinely wanted you to enjoy your stay in their city.
They were proud of their heritage
Sharing stories of their history and the culture's survival through time.
A few more days removed.
I recognize how much new historical knowledge I gained while there.
Given the opportunity, the Big Easy could awaken something in you too.

# The Desert

Stranded in a creative desert

Words escape me

Nothing to show on paper

Wisps of a scene dance through my mind,
then disappear before the words land in my story.

This journey is unsettling

Leaving me feeling ill at ease

Besides being dry and barren, deserts are often hot
To escape the dullness of these empty days
We went to a concert.

The outdoor setting provided a great escape from the heat

Venue was filled with people enjoying themselves

An evening breeze blew in from the ocean

A lovely time was had

A threesome unlocked a creative muse within me
The characters, were all – characters
I was certain there was a story beneath the surface

Back home after a lovely evening of music by the shore,
a short story was born.

# Sleep

Why are you elusive?
My eyelids are heavy
Yawning frequently.

I lay down
Then toss and turn
Comfortable, I am not.

Diminished rest takes its toll.
My mind is dull
And my spirit heavy.
Sleep where are you?
Why have you run away from me?

# Everything Happens For a Reason

Really?
Or is life predetermined?
Do you make your own destiny
Or does coincidence exist?
Do things work out the way they are supposed to
Or have we learned to make the best of things?

It depends upon one's basic philosophy.
You either think the world is out to get you
Or
The world is yours to explore.

I try to find an adventure around every corner.
Most days this attitude serves me well.

So for me,
I would say most things happen for a reason.

Until I get up from the wrong side of the bed,
Then I find grey clouds hanging in the air.

Gratefully, those days are few and far between.

# Fear

You can't see me, but you sense my presence.
Yeah, that's right.
I'm here, breathing down your neck,
Whispering in your ear,
Sending images to your mind.

You think you can get away,
But you're wrong.
I've got a firm grip on you
And I'm not letting go.

That's right, question if going on vacation is really safe;
Question if you'll be alright if you spend that money;
Question what they are really saying about you when you're not there.

You muddle through your day pretending I'm not here.
Then you lay down and I flood your mind with thoughts.
What happens if the lab results are bad?
What happens if ruffians move into the neighborhood?
What happens if the power goes out?

And so, you toss and turn. I've chased sleep away from you.
There's no rest for the weary, and I keep you weary.
Yes, I do.
When you think you can relax,
I remind you of something else to worry about.

If I can keep your mind on all these questions
You might not notice
Your friend standing over there,
Cheering you on
Lifting you in prayer.
You may not see love in action.

Oh, Love—get out of here.
You, Love, are crowding my space.
Don't go whispering words into her ears
As you squeeze me out of her mind.

Stop! Love, Stop!
I've heard Love casts out fear.
I'm losing my hold on her mind.
I'm diminishing,
I'm fading,
I'm gone....

Perfect Love casts out all fear.

# Wait! I Thought It Was Dead!

Wait! I thought it was dead.
Words lost their ability
to inspire and spur one onto good deeds.
Instead, they were only
sowing division and anxiety.
This change caused me to lose hope I might impact
another with my words.
Words were becoming dead.
Retreating from my writing practice left me feeling ungrounded.
What was my purpose?
Perhaps arrogantly
I thought I could say things which would impact another.
Hope, my hope,
like wings, was flying away.
Purpose is so core to one's self esteem
And mine was sinking.
Unexpectedly, you sent a photo and a text.
The photo was a screenshot of a page from
**Clouds, Dreams & Fantasy**
A page, I had written.
The text was how it had spoken to you,
and that you enjoyed it.
Your reaction deeply touched my heart
And the words powerfully reminded me—
I may not change what is going on around me
but I can Watch My Mind
Which allows me to change what is
Going on in my own life.
You proved, the power of words is not dead!

## Watch Your Mind

*Clouds, Dreams & Fantasy Copyright 2023 by AppleWood Press*

Watch your mind... As individuals, we tend to forget the power of the mind and forget the power we can exercise over the mind.

Watch your mind... What lessons are there to learn? The past creeps in and tries to steal the peace we've learned to live with, replacing it instead with memories of pain and heartache.

Oh, watch your mind... You can command those thoughts to depart and instead focus on positive or joyful thoughts for today. There is beauty which exists around us. If we take occasion to search for it, we'll find it. It may be as grand as the sky lit up with the radiant colors of the sun saying goodbye at day's end, or as small as a perfect flax flower with its open head waving in the morning sunshine. Beauty abounds.

Watch your mind... No lectures, no speeches, no judgment—instead, allow forgiveness and acceptance to flow through you to those around you. Share the joy of living with those you come in contact with. Speak words of encouragement and life to others. Let your words tell others who they can be. Speak life!

# Power of Prayer

Shrouded in pain.
Feelings hurt,
Draw inward to protect self.

Wrapped in agony.
From deep within
My heart is calling me
To forgive.

Scream out

No!

Not fair!

Don't want to.

Need relief.

Provided no details.
Simply, Requested prayer—
...for a change of heart

Peace settled in, reminding me
I am loved.

My beloved comforts me.
...lifts me up
...reminds me whose I am
...what truth is.

# Hidden in Plain Sight

The topic for the week was Miracles.
I was elated.
Emotions evoked were upbeat and energizing.
I was sure it would be easy and fun to write this week.

My brain was abuzz with images.
No story came.

I struggled.
Should this be about a personal miracle
or one I simply witnessed?
I've so many grand miracles to tell of
Yet, there is so much wonder and amazement in every day.
Would it be offensive to share personal stories?
Could it seem trite to write of the small miracles which touch my soul
daily?
My mind whirred.
The sun came up morning after morning
with no words to share what miracles mean to me.
My saffron crocus is blooming
and daily I go to harvest the tiny red stigma.
I'm still awed to be able to grow this spice I so enjoy using,
and amazed I live on a property
which produces so many things to eat.
I enjoy a leisurely morning with my husband
soaking in the views and cooler temperatures this season brings.
The internet allows a face-to-face communication
with a friend separated by geographical distance.
Other friends gather
to share and enjoy our common faith. Sometimes
we encourage one another through difficult days.
Soon, so very soon,
as a family, we'll celebrate the 17th birthday of a grandson
who miraculously recovered from a heart transplant
and has been graciously granted extended life.
The sun goes down.
The stars
just as the clouds by day
simply hang suspended in the sky.

Perchance you'll be fortunate to witness
the death of a star as it rapidly explodes
and disappears in the night sky.
I have lived many days
traveled to many different places
have friends scattered around the globe
and have memories which exceed anything
I could have imagined in my youth.
I know I am loved.
I know love,
and I love others.
Life has brought many surprises,
some of which I wouldn't wish on anyone,
yet with confidence, I can say,
"Life is Good!"

Still, no good story for miracles.

I read the following quote from C.S. Lewis
which summarizes my dilemma well.
*Miracles are a retelling in small letters*
*of the very same story*
*which is written across the whole world*
*in letters too large for some of us to see.*

# People of the Night

Unknown people dropped off at a major international airport.
All having hours to await their departure,
All unwittingly becoming—
People of the Night

The environment provided an interesting zone for people-watching.
Some, like us, went to an all-night steak restaurant.
Some, not us, once there, fell asleep at their table,
We enjoyed dinner at midnight.
Then walked, noting which shops were open,
People entering through security.
Others, also walking.
Still others settled in for the night in seating areas.
We too, would soon join them.

Being newcomers to this traveling group,
People of the Night
We found some stretched out on the seating
Where this comfort was allowed.
Many dozed.
I recognized how unprepared we were.
It was chilly.
We had no sweatsuits.
No blankets.
No extra sweaters or outer wear.

Restful sleep eluded me as I struggled to get comfortable.
But rest, I did.
I felt secure.
People remained within their own groups.
Airport security quietly moved around,
Or periodically stopped to sit in various seating areas.
Slowly, the environment came to life as
Pilots and airplane staff arrived.
Transformed,
The People of the Night
Packed up their belongings
Appearing as any other weary traveler,
Eager to arrive at their destination.

Morning employees were chipper and helpful.

We enjoyed an excellent breakfast, including steamy beverages
before boarding our last flight.
The sleep which eluded me all night
arrived before the plane was airborne.

Days later
I would learn
the airport atmosphere was entirely different
at the end of a weekend day.

Linda L. Flynn

# SEASONAL

# Ready or Not

Ready or not—
In front of me, the doorway loomed.
Unknown uncertainties were on the other side.
Reluctance and hesitation were foreign to me
for the task which lay ahead.

Ready or not—
Time propelled me through the entranceway.
Another decade
loomed ahead of me.

What adventures would find me?
What new discoveries await me?
Memories of previous decades kept distracting me,
Reminding me life has been full of encounters.
Besides many successes
Earlier decades were filled with striving.
In a hurry to get somewhere,
Anywhere, just away from the NOW.
Better was always ahead
or so life predicted.

Ready or not—
Growth came.
  teen years
  adult years
  motherhood
  learning years, always learning years
  singlehood
  married life
  grandkids
  self-acceptance
  self confidence
  awareness of life, self, others, and God's hidden hand
  weaving in and throughout life.

And now
Ready or not—-
This decade brings the realization that most striving is for naught.

Living is in the little things.
Simple pleasures enjoyed with another.
Quiet moments reflecting on the beauty of this life.
Often times, I'm distracted by the noise of the day
   cultural noise
   political noise
   geopolitical noise
   the continual encouragement to strive
Always striving.

Ready or not—-
I'm here in this seventh decade
Facing an uncertain future.
Confident of who my God is
and where my source of strength comes from.
Knowing it is okay,
  to be a little slower
  to be invisible to some,
  to purposely enjoy those around me
  to appreciate the beauty of nature and the magic of the night sky
  to let things happen
  to be grateful for the gift of another day.

Ready or not—
The time is now,

It is what I have been given.

## Taking Chances.

Isn't that what life is about?
Another journey around the sun.
Out with the old, In with the new
What does it mean to you?

The sun is shining, lighting up the land around me
Blue sky intensifying the colors of the day.
A light breeze blows, beckoning me outdoors
Just as the new year beckons me to throw aside caution
And enter with wild abandon into the unknown future

The future –
...another year older
...deeper understanding
...new challenges and adventures await
...refining or honing skills
...giving up unrealistic expectations
...savoring the gift of another day
...tenderly holding precious memories
...valuing relationships
...acknowledging more, the power of God's love
...and learning how to walk frequently in this love

It is all a chance.
A chance I take willingly.
Out with the old, In with the new,
What does it mean to you?

## Traditions

The word evokes many thoughts,
Different for each of us.
Impact of these thoughts is equally dissimilar.
Some individuals become melancholy,
Others upbeat and joyful.

The word suggests something one can count on.
Yet in truth, traditions reflect change.

My granny baked an abundant assortment of cookies,
Enjoyed by all, with each of us having our favorites.
I took my favorite and ensured it was made every year.
Thus, my children were introduced to my favorite for the Christmas season,
Then, their children delighted in these same little delicate sweets.

Each of these children have carried some traditions from my home to their own,
Adding new twists and turns creating something unique for their families.

No littles at my house for the holidays.
Yet these little green trees still get pulled from the oven to be enjoyed by others.
An adult grandchild, with children of her own
Requested her gift be a box of these cookies for her family.

I smile.
How my granny would be honored to know
These little gems she so readily baked
are still being enjoyed five generations later.

A tradition continues.

# Up in Flames

Ahh,
can you hear it?

2024 is groaning under the weight
of all the happenings of the year.

Too many happenings to list here.

Are you groaning as well?

Here's the cure...

Slip into your snuggly warm jammies,
or comfortable sweats,
grab a warm cup of your favorite steamy brew,
take your preferred throw or blanket
and settle in front of the fire.

A big roaring fire.

Listen to the crackles as little sparks pop from the blaze.
Watch the flames of the fire rise,
rise to the sky or up the firebox.

Give your thoughts of the year
to those flames.

Let the flames take the weight of 2024 with them.
Rising into the heights of the heavens,
then dissipating in the air.

Allow the smoke to fill your nostrils
like incense, purifying your soul.

Watch the flames licking the logs
slowly turning the surfaces into
glowing
red

searing
heat sources.
Soak in this heat.
Sit quietly and let the weight of 2024
escape from your body.

Soak in enough of the heat
that you need to toss the blanket aside.

Quiet your mind.
Think about the flames making the logs smaller.
Let your stressful thoughts shrink as well.
Breathe deeply.
A new morning is coming.
2025 will arrive like a new babe.
Welcome it into your life—
Uncorrupted,
Renewed,
Original.

From the ashes of 2024, let something new
be created in you this coming year.

Embrace the possibility of new beginnings.
Wrap them around yourself like the blanket you
previously tossed.

Hold your head high and enter the new year.

# Deck the Halls

Drag containers from storage closet.
Items stowed away from last Christmas
Lie wrapped in tissue, carefully packed in these boxes.

Fire is crackling and flames dancing
In preparation of merriment.

With the opening of each box and the unwrapping of each item
Memories spring to mind.
All those years of exchanging ornaments reveal remembrances of friends
and family.
I smile, as peacefulness fills my soul.
This tree, during the holiday season represents my lifetime.

And what a lifetime it has been
Crossing oceans
Living in multiple communities
Moving more times than I can count.
Memories abound from each of these locations.
Yet it's the friends which exist in all those habitations,
And our camaraderie that fills my life with encouragement and joy
Which I savor the most.

Ah, friends.
Years and physical distance may have us parted,
But this evening you are here with me,
Celebrating another holiday season.

# NATURE

# Returning

Amazing trip
Renewed and strengthened friendships
Days filled with activities and interactions

Below the surface covid tensions linger
Invasion of Ukraine triggers new anxieties
Time to depart arrives as exhaustion set in
Uneventful long flight lands in San Diego
A welcome familial face greets us,
To take us home.

March and winter rains green the countryside
Quick trip on the interstate to our exit
Winding roads through mountains and hills
Trees arching over the hilly road and our driveway
All acting like flags marking the pathway.

The house sits,
A welcome beacon speaking
"Welcome, welcome"
Us like strangers, but not,
Walk around the gardens closest to the house
Soaking in the beauty
Amazed by the growth of two months.

Casual conversation with son-in-law before he departs,
Leaving us in the quietness of our house

We walk the space
Acquainting our senses with each room.
Like a warm drink and fire in the hearth,
Home provides welcome comfort.

# Nature's Preparations

Packed and prepared to leave.
Blurry-eyed
I grab my purse,
Sit and buckle in.
Relative quietness hangs upon the town.
Entering the freeway
Ribbons of white or red lights
Stream down the roadway.
Who would have known so many
Would be on the road long before light?

Dawn
Presents the first signs of the day to come.
Heavy clouds hang
On the mountaintops.
Light peeking through
Revealing the foothills
Beneath the shrouded peaks.
Spots of pink adorn the clouds.
Traffic intensifies.
At times
Its pace like a crawl
Resembles more of a parking lot than streamers.

Drawn back to the coast—
We stand on the rocky shore
Listen to the crashing waves
Watch sea lions bob and play
Survey crumbling walls
Succumbed to an earlier hurricane.
The air
The light
The beauty of the sea
On such a day as this.

To town we travel
Where we traipse
From one art shop to another.
Early dinner on Main Street

Then off to the lodge.
With other guests of the establishment
We enjoy a hot drink
A fire
And live entertainment.
Later
We fall into bed
Drifting off to sleep.
Morning arrives.
Opening the shutters
I found the marine layer rolling in
Mingled with the Spanish moss
Hanging on the trees.
The shadows and mist
Changed the local landscape,
Creating a foreboding atmosphere.

# New Day, New Beginnings

The morning light was not so bright.
Pulling back the curtains and stepping onto the deck
I see the marine layer has followed the valley
Inland
And crept up the hill to my house
Leaving the world in a cloudy haze
Devoid of the vibrant colors of life.
Moisture settled on tabletops
Plants and the walkways.
The air was cool
Bordering on being cold
Driving me back indoors.
Busying myself in the house
I failed to notice when the sun came out
And slowly drove the marine layer from the valley
And back to the sea.

This midday sun beckoned me back outdoors
Where the moisture on the plants
Now warmed by the sun worked its own magic.
Orange trees loaded with small white pearls
Waiting to burst forth into star blooms,
Gracefully hung on the tree.
For those five petal blooms already open,
The combination of moisture and sun
Releases the most intoxicating perfume
Wafting through the air.
Breathing in this fragrance clears one's mind.

How fitting.
I learned orange blossoms are regularly celebrated for their
purity and beauty.
They often represent fertility, purity, and good fortune.
In some cultures, they are associated with new beginnings or weddings.
The clearing of my mind
Calls forth for both new beginnings
And good fortune

What would be the impact
if we could pump this fragrance
of fresh orange blossoms
Around the world?
Do you think anyone would notice?

# What Makes You Smile

This makes me smile.
Sunrise reflecting against the western slopes where the
Morning marine layer hangs in the valleys beneath the sunshine.
Shade on my patio
Allowing me to sit outdoors and witness this display of nature.
Listening to the various birds as they greet the day.

Blue fills the sky as the light chases away the marine layer.
Heat creeps onto the patio.
Without the umbrella, I would be chased inside.
But instead, I languish, enjoying my brew.
Smiling as I anticipate another beautiful day.
What makes you smile?

## What the Sun Feels Like

The long dark winter has passed.
Small green shoots poke through the earth with the
promise of blooms to follow.
Yellow
White
Purple.

Oh, please allow them to come quickly.
I'm weary of the dark and cold.
Longing for the spark of life to come,
Desiring blue skies and warmer days

Over the edge of the horizon
The sun breaks forth.
Bright light emitting from the fiery hot ball
Warming the cold hard earth
And my cold body.
I sit in the sun and savor the heat slowly radiating within me.
The birds chirp,
Fluttering from branch to branch
Heralding the arrival of spring.

Yes, I sit back,
allowing the sun to fall on my face.
Smiling as I welcome the arrival of spring,
the rebirth of living things.

## Handstamped

Seemingly at the very edge of the world,
Steps from the deck descend the rocks
Then end.
High tide rolls in
Obliterating the bottom steps
And sand below.
Waves crash upon the rocks
Spraying high into the air
Then dropping on the deck
before returning to the sea.
Other waves roll in
Splashing against the house.
The tide recedes
and the ever-constant cycle repeats.
The sun comes up and then,
The sun goes down with
God's majesty on full display...
As His handstamped sunset ends each blue day.

# Coming Home

*(Published on The Galway Review site on 9/20/2023)*

Winding roads through mountains and hills
Arched trees dapple the light of the final ascent
The house awaits us
Arrayed by splendor of nature, it sits.

Car parks
We debark

Like strangers, but not...
The symphony begins.

Steady beat of the house declaring
Welcome Home!
Welcome Home!

Eye candy of the property draws us to walk our land
Assorted shades and textures of green dance before our eyes.

Bougainvillea stand proud
Their finery like a fountain falling back to the ground.

Distinct fragrance of the giant Eucalyptus fills the air.
Tiny ice plants cover a slope in soft lavender
Releasing their soft sweet fragrance in small bursts.

Grape vines show signs of their annual rebirth
Cacti soften their prickly exterior with magnificent blooms.

Round the corner
Awakened, the sleeping rose bed waits, awash with color
Saying "we missed you!"

Surveying the hillside below the patio
And the mountains beyond

We stand, arm in arm and smile
As with any great trip

The welcome comfort of home greets us.

# The Sea

*life's journey*

The sound of the sea
  in a small voice
  beckoned to me.

I heeded not the call
  and became known
  as wife and mother to all.

To the heartland I returned
  where I gave my children wings
  and the title 'wife' was burned.

Many years passed
  and in the same heartland I found
  the love of my life at last.

And by the sea
  we exchanged our vows with no thought
  of the call which once beckoned me.

## Rose Garden

The rose garden came with the house
Neglected, yet holding the promise of showy colors
soft, delicate petals
and lush fragrances

I enjoyed the lingering blooms before winter set in
Then allowed the gardener to prune
All these months later
I've learned how roses thirst
They now drink regularly,
each from their own spigot off the irrigation system

I've learned roses hunger
Bi-monthly, they each receive their nutrient rich feast

And now I've watched fresh growth
showy colors
soft delicate petals
and inhale lush fragrances

# Southern California Living

Compared to other locations
One can be confused about seasons here

There are four seasons
Just different from other areas
The transitions are more subtle

Something blooms in each season
Creating an abundance of color within the garden

Sounds from bird choirs and choruses fill the air
Each singing a unique song

Winter brings the rains which water the earth
And begin the growing cycle

Spring arrives
May Grey arrives with most mornings
Pulling the marine layer like a duvet onto the land
By midday the heat from above has caused this blanket
To be tossed aside
Revealing the sun which shines on the parcel
Breezes blow in from the ocean
Causing the tree branches to dance and sway
Plants thrive in this atmosphere

We soon say goodbye to May Grey
Only to usher in June Gloom
Which is mostly a repeat of the May pattern

Summer brings warmer days
Still pleasant due to the ocean breezes
With this change in the season
Comes an influx of travelers

Autumn unleashes heat in full force
Driving many to spend days indoors
Or escape to the ocean or some cooler destination
The land dries as many plants depend on external water

Due to school schedules activities change
Traffic lessens and many of the tourists have returned to their nests

October gives way to November
When moderate temperatures return
The shorter days remind us winter is coming
And maybe the rain

What's to dislike about this?

# Autumn evening

Gone is summer
With the arrival of
Chilly evenings

Comfy chair
A time of reflection
Designed for me

A warm drink
Snuggly blanket
Fire crackling

Good book
Safe and secure
Warm at home

Soft background music
Words on the page
Carry me away

## Beach chair

Waves roll onto the shore
Tumbling in their wake
Shells, rocks, and other treasures
roll on the beach as the waves
Recede back into the ocean

Treasures line the shore
Beachcombers walk the wet sand
each looking for what speaks to their heart

Some carefully selecting items
Others scooping up hands full
Each dropping their finds into beach totes

Imagine with me
Sea trinkets roll onto the beach
Each shell or rock holding a memory
my mother reading me stories
my grandmother baking my favorite cookies
my grandfather gruffly saying we need blackberry brandy
to cure that cough
my father gently teaching me how to ice skate
my elderly neighbor taking me under her wing, becoming a life mentor
my first date
my first child
and so on, the memories line the shores
Then I watch, as shells are picked up by a beachcomber
each held in hand
turned over and peered at before being
dropped into their tote or back on the beach

Do they see the memories, or just a sea trinket
What fabled stories lay scattered on the beach
Are others stealing your memories or sharing them

Linda L. Flynn

# CULTURAL

## All Roads Lead To

you asked
how did I end up here
this was never my plan

how do you tell someone
usually it is the collective results
of millions of little decisions and steps
*leading us to the truth*
*that all roads lead to right where you find yourself*

those words tend to land hard
admittedly there are some things caused by
genetics
geography
environment
status
politics
disease
natural catastrophe
accident

yet even after those explanations
how we react is the sum of our own choices
each choice opens or closes another door
and sets us on a trajectory

we may not recognize the result as a conscious choice
*leading us to the truth*
*that all roads lead to right where you find yourself*

none of us get to remain where we find ourselves
every day there are new choices and decisions
resulting in new roads to travel
*leading us to the truth*
*that all roads lead to right where you will find yourself*

we see another only in a snapshot of time
often with no knowledge of the roads they travelled
to arrive at the destination where you find them
blink
and they will be somewhere else

nothing is static
change is constant
though not always welcome
unwelcome as change may be
and the resulting choices
*even these choices lead us to the truth*
*that all roads lead to right where you will find yourself*

# Dawning of Day or Darkness of Night

Which is it?
These times proclaim both options.
Depending upon your perspective
And personal inclinations

Twilight presents that in-between time
Not quite something yet, but
Promises of something yet to come

Contingent upon your lens
You may see the beauty
Bounding into the future and
Revel in the peacefulness you anticipate.
Or you may enter gingerly,
Fearful of what awaits you.

So it is. With both the
Transition from day to night
Or night to day, just as in life
Changes always occur.

The world holds its breath, waiting to see
What will emerge from this transition

There are glimpses from both sides.
See where you fall


Twilight

In-between...

Twilight

The experience surrounds us

Where will you be found?

# Habits

*Clouds, Dreams & Fantasy Copyright 2023 by AppleWood Press*

Habits creep in like stalkers at night
We awake and find them amongst us

So goes the way of the news
Read for interest or to be informed
Look for more complete details
Shock value captivates attention

Research
Then repeat
And repeat
Peace disrupted
Habit revealed

I long to return to consuming news
On a "need to know" basis

Yet still struggle with the question
How to be informed yet not addicted

## July 1, 2024

Flip the calendar page
A new month is upon us.
Surprisingly,
Fresh changes in my attitude

I found myself stuck.
Dreading the direction of our country's future
Questioning how this all plays out as a Christian.
Fearing the loss of the world as I've always known it.

Revelation!
Change is inevitable.
It always happens.
No one can stop it or hold it back.
Attempting to do so leaves one
irrelevant
out of touch
frustrated
difficult to communicate with
old
cranky
ultimately lonely, and sad.

Three colliding statements or thoughts
Merged in my mind
Thus, changing me.

"We are no longer fighting to keep democracy,
we've already moved past democracy."

"We are in the midst of a civil war,
not we're headed toward, but we are in."

Christians exist all around the world,
many in despicable conditions.
Yet they are there, and their faith thrives.

The question for me becomes:
how do I continue to live my faith and witness to God's truth,
even as everything around me is changing?

The focus shifted
It is no longer how
will the changes in our culture affect me,
or how to stop the changes,
but how
will I continue to worship and
serve the God
I love no matter what the circumstances?

# Different Meanings

Same words
Different meanings
"Concern for the future of our country"

To her
Control by political party will determine future fate
Recession to come like nothing we've seen before
Forced Covid vaccines or forfeiture of social security benefits
Loss of parental control over children's vaccine status

To me
Those issues will be small problems compared to what is thrust upon us
Autocracy which strips the right to vote
Eliminating the voice or will of the people.
Education which neglects to teach children to think or reason
Generating little robots who only say "yes"

Each agreed polarization of news contributes

To me
Often avoiding news
Affront to her I would do so

To me
Our responsibility to validate what we've heard on the news
Often requires researching old historical documents
I'm weary of the time and effort this takes.
I'm saddened by what this research reveals
Of the untruths discovered and failures of reporting

To her
Agrees on process and responsibility
But admits no time for this task.
Determines anger is the cultural problem.

To me
Agree anger is a problem.
Long for being able to discuss differences
Without anger and vitriol
Long for people wanting to work together.

To her
Agrees those were superior practices employed at better times.

Personal Reflections
Grateful we could talk.
Saddened how much of populous shares her thoughts.

Late thoughts
For me
Acknowledgment of what facilitates change—
Affecting the mind of one person at a time.
Exhaustion sets in.
My question
Do I have the energy?
Thoughts turn to children, grandchildren, future generations.
I ponder what others endured
For freedoms I've enjoyed.
Dare I sit down and allow the future to be so altered
With so much at stake?

# Tension

### *Pre 2024 elections*

Tension
It hangs in the air like a heavy cloak.
Daily
The airwaves blare stories more bizarre than the day before.

Natural disasters occur at an unprecedented pace.
One hasn't recovered from the last before the next arrives.
Some use these unfortunate events to stir political unrest,
to the detriment of those involved.

Life seems to be lived on a tightrope at this time.
One side, being that of tension and the other of being incensed
or outraged by whatever came through the news.
People are moving around cautiously,
not wanting to push another off the tightrope
for fear of what their reactions will be.

Foolishly, or not, we will travel in this time and space.
Totally unaware and unprepared for what we may encounter.
Never in my life has so much ridden on an election.
Never have both sides expressed the same fears,
yet for completely different reasons.

# Spinning

## *June 2024*

There is a heaviness in the air
Hanging in suspension
It weighs down my spirit
Waiting for the next....

Next, what???

No one knows what they are waiting for.
Emotions are strained in all directions.

Divisiveness is a primary tool.
It has been wielded well
Leaving people wary of others

The news spins stories
Conjuring feelings of...

Accountability
Anger
Apathy
Celebration
Disbelief
Disappointment
Exhaustion
Fear
Jubilation
Punishment
Relief
Retribution
Sadness
Terror

Beyond all these emotions
Is the sense we are losing something important
It seems like there is no road back.
This experiment of a republic is all I've known

Now it appears as though I'm standing on a precipice
The ground beneath me is unstable

Sadly, people on both sides of this abyss
Express the same feelings.
Yet because the paths to this thought are so divergent
There is no common resolution.

As this world continues to spin out of control
My faith reminds me
God is not caught off guard by any of this.
We've been told there will be troubles in this world
So why am I surprised when I know my strength comes from Him?

For me, I know I need to keep returning,
Turning and returning to His truths.

# Exhaustion

two different news cycles spew words at us
they come in rapid bursts
much like machine gun fire

in truth the wreckage they leave behind
is also similar to what is found
in the wake of machine gun fire

sources having printed words unflattering
to the current administration
have future access denied

actions that would have been unthinkable
a few short years ago
are on full display for the world to witness

the effect of the wreckage
like a broad overarching stroke from a loaded paintbrush
is leaving evidence of having been here

people's lives are being upended
some in very tangible ways
others in their more secondary rituals

in my community we walk around
with smiles on our faces
leaving me to wonder if I alone am concerned

being singular in seeing these events or wondering
if conspiracy theories have invaded my mind
causing me to see these bad things

I attempt to avoid the news
yet some magnetic force pulls me
I struggle

looking for positive things to counter
the troubling information
I pull away

yet enough of the dross
hits and clings to my mind and soul
causing stories of unthinkable things to swirl

in and out of my brain
over and over again
the repetitive motion of this practice

wears on my body and psyche
leaving few resources to address the matters
of daily living

is that the actual goal of these crazy days
to wear people down
to make them incapable of life

stress intensifies
stealing restful sleep
awakening to a new morning

which only repeats the cycle of the previous day
exhaustion settles in the body and mind
eyelids are heavy and breathing becomes laborious

wear the people down with one news story after another
each so bizarre and unbelievable that they become incredibly exhausted
and cannot recognize what is happening to their culture

to all the things they thought
they knew the stable forces of
their civilization

then the actual changes can be implemented
will we be able to withstand this assault
on life as we know it

# Challenged

*the landscape shifted*
*an ominousness lingers in the air*
*things will change…*
*…or will they?*

Oxygen is sucked from the airwaves
News stations drone on endlessly
Rarely does a report contain any deviations.

At my house, the news is not on
My choice is the written word
And even that is an endless barrage of expression
Most reporting different tweaks of the same event

My eyes blur
My brain hurts
My emotions are taut
My body is weary and tense

In truth,
I can control what I ingest when I'm home
I just need to discipline myself
It's when I'm out.
Many consume a constant feed of audio or visual slop
Produced by those who profess to provide news.

Some exhibit glee when they hear of an event
Which harms their perceived foes
I lack a response.
My heart hurts
I recognize I must learn to navigate this unfamiliar terrain.

Moving with the steady stream of vehicles
The countryside flashes past the window
No time to focus.
It all becomes a blur.
What was not flying by was within the automobile.

Surprised
I witnessed myself speaking out.
No judgement, just a simple request
After what seemed like an endless eternity,
I asked the driver of the vehicle if we could turn on music
Or turn off the reporting.

It had been nothing but repetitive.
We'd all heard the events
The constant retelling had the effect of waterboarding.
I felt myself getting tense
Agitation building within me.
Still, early in the day's outing

The simple request resulted in music.
Oldies
Certainly, more upbeat than what previously filled the atmosphere

Mine was not a hard request
There was no judgement
No explanation
Just a simple question

The result was a change for all of us
The day was pleasant
We spent it within a presidential library
History surrounded us.

Now, reflecting on the day
I see myself changing.
Slowly, I see my inner strength building.
Can I continue to cultivate this sense of control and peace?

# The Calm Before the Storm

The day
Is like any normal day.
Until it is not.
The air becomes still,
Too still.
Yet man may not notice.

All animal and insect activity ceased
As though they vanished from the earth.
What innate sense do they have
Which alerted them to this coming storm?

It all happens so fast.
The sky becomes dark.
Clouds build.
Suddenly a dark grey funnel cloud forms on the horizon,
Rising into the heavens,
Spinning towards earth,
With its tail whipping and flapping as it moves.
The winds pick up.

Seemingly without notice
Items are lifted into the air
Then flung down in some other location.

Even vehicles are hurled through space.
Walls crash
And yet a nearby structure sustains no damage.
There is no explanation
For what is ravaged,
And what is spared.

The tornado is fast,
Wreaking havoc as it throws itself into space.
Gone,
As quickly as it arrived,
Leaving wreckage in its wake.

Those animals and creatures who took cover
Slowly reappear.
The sounds of nature return,
Augmented by the wailing
Of those whose lives lay in ruin.

How did man not see this coming?

Yet this seems to be the nature of man.
The signs are on the horizon.
Visible,
Yet he sees them not.
He becomes easily distracted
Or swayed by charismatic personalities.
Promises of things he has never previously considered
Are suddenly important.
Fears are played upon until he is sure there is a threat
To his way of life.
This charismatic person presents himself as the answer to all.
Logic would dictate
One cannot deal with all.
>    *Still, a man hears what he wants to hear*
>    *...and disregards the rest*
From *The Boxer by Paul Simon*
Words of warning hidden in a song from 1968
Yet man has no recollection.

So here we find ourselves.
Where some revel in glee
When they hear of one of their pet fears being addressed,
Yet overlook the next news item.
They fail to see the magnitude of the changes being hurled at us
With such rapid succession.
There is no time to comprehend the full scope of what is happening.
Unprepared for the sudden storm which is upon us
The enormity
Like none we've seen in our lifetimes.
People looking from one to another for shelter
Only to find the fortresses of our culture destroyed
And replaced with a modern-day bastille.

What will arise from the ashes?

## About the Author

Since early childhood, books and the written word have fascinated Linda. Stories carried her away and fostered a desire to understand cultures, people and life. Her dream of traveling became part of her reality. She has lived in many places within the United States and Europe. Linda believes, 'Life is the journey,' and that is what she writes about. In her words; you will find relationships, nature, healing hurts, beauty, hopefulness, struggles, and faith. All of these are essential elements in our lives.

The primary hope she has for her readers is that her stories and words pull them in, and that they find a kinship or connection in her writings. She wants them to be inspired to realize others share similar feelings or experiences. So, connections both to the characters and then connections to those in the readers' circle are important, so they will know their lives matter.

Her books display a variety of writing styles, yet each assessed something important to her and of interest to the larger community.

Find her work at amazon.com/author/lindalflynn_words

Or connect with her on her blog site at www.journeytotheheights.com

Stop by her blog site and say "hi," or share your thoughts with her there.

Linda L. Flynn

Thank you for reading *Twilight ...the in-between.* I hope you enjoyed it. If you did, please help other readers find this book:

1. The Kindle version of this book is lendable, so send it to a friend you think might like it so they can discover me, too. (Terms of lending established by "Lending for Kindle.")
2. Help other people find this book by writing a review on Amazon. Other than word of mouth, reviews are the primary way people find books. I appreciate your helping me in this way.
3. Check out my website: journeytotheheights.com
4. Follow me on either my blogsite (journeytotheheights.com) or my Facebook page, (Linda Flynn).

www.ingramcontent.com/pod-product-compliance
Lightning Source LLC
Chambersburg PA
CBHW060235180626
46813CB00007B/3094